Dedication

To Elysa, my love.

J. Alan Dawkins

In a beautiful, busy meadow full of animals and bugs, life was happy and friendly. Butterflies, ants, and many other creatures worked together to make their home awesome. Benny the Butterfly was super strong and nice. He helped the ants carry leaves back to their home. Lucy the Ladybug had colorful spots that made everyone happy just by looking at her. Sally the Snail moved slowly, but she was really hard-working, making sure all the plants were healthy. On sunny days, you could hear bees buzzing as they collected sweet nectar, crickets chirping songs, and fireflies laughing and talking. Everyone said 'please' and 'thank you' just like you hear the sound of leaves shaking and water flowing in the stream nearby.

But there was one bug who didn't fit in, and that was Manny the Mantis. Manny always wanted to do things his own way, even if it wasn't polite. If bugs were waiting in line for dewdrops in the morning, Manny would jump to the front. At parties like the Big Spring Picnic, he'd knock over cups filled with sweet drinks and just walk away without cleaning up. He never said 'please' or 'thank you.'

Whenever Manny showed up, the happy feeling in the air would go away. People would stop talking, stop smiling, and give each other looks that said, "Uh-oh, here comes trouble." Manny didn't seem to know he was making everyone feel this way, and it looked like something would have to change soon.

Everyone in the field helped each other. Ants shared snacks with spiders, fireflies led the way for bugs who were lost, and ladybugs let others use their pretty shells for art. But Manny was like a rock thrown into a calm pond, making ripples that messed up the peace and happiness.

One sunny day, a group of bugs were hanging out near a pretty new flower. Benny the Butterfly was talking about how everything in nature works together when Manny the Mantis shouted, "Flowers are boring! Let's talk about something cool!" The other bugs looked at each other but stayed quiet. They didn't want to start a fight.

A few nights later, Lucy, the Ladybug, was telling a special story about her family long ago. Everyone was listening closely, but then Manny started messing with the leaves and mumbling to himself. He ruined the cozy feeling everyone had.

Another time, Terrence the Tarantula was showing the younger bugs how to make cool silk patterns. Just as Terrence was about to share a special trick, Manny yelled, "Is this going to take forever?

I've got better stuff to do!" The bugs around him sighed and couldn't focus anymore. Then, the crickets had a music show where they'd all chirp together to make a relaxing tune. But Manny thought that was the perfect time to make his own loud, off-key sounds. The crickets got mixed up, and the music show was ruined.

Now, bugs in the field were really getting frustrated. They started saying to each other, "We have to do something about Manny. He's not nice to anyone!"

The bugs were thinking really hard. Should they stop inviting Manny to hang out? Maybe they should have a big meeting to talk about what's going on. Everyone loved living in a friendly place and wanted to keep it that way, but Manny kept spoiling the fun.

It was clear - things had to change. Manny was close to being left out by everyone, and it seemed like he didn't even know that people were getting upset with him.

3

The Great Nectar Feast was coming up, and it was one of the most fun times in the meadow! All the bugs looked forward to it every year. This year was extra special because a Golden Blossom flower was going to bloom, making the feast even yummier.

Manny was really pumped for the feast. He was already planning how to get to the best nectar first. He couldn't wait to taste the special nectar from the Golden Blossom. But then, something surprising happened. Every bug got a leaf invitation except for Manny.

Feeling confused and sad, Manny went to Benny the Butterfly. "Hey, Benny, did you forget to give me an invite to the Great Nectar Feast?"

Benny sighed and said, "No, Manny. It wasn't forgotten. The bugs decided not to invite you this year."

Manny was shocked. "What? Why?" Benny answered in a kind but serious way, "You've upset a lot of friends here. From being too loud when Lucy was telling her story to messing up Wendy's art, you haven't been nice. Everyone thinks you won't make the feast a happy time."

Manny felt like he'd been struck by lightning. For the first time, he understood that his actions had made others unhappy. He looked around at all the bugs talking, laughing, and getting ready for the feast. For the first time, he felt all alone. His heart felt heavy as he watched everyone having fun and getting excited. All of it was something he was now missing out on. He felt really, really sorry like someone had just taken the air out of him.

Manny knew he had to make things right. Not just to go to the feast but to really be a part of the friendly meadow he had always lived in but never really appreciated.

Still feeling really sad about being left out, Manny walked around the meadow not really knowing where to go. His mind was filled with sorry thoughts. That's when he saw Gloria, an older butterfly who was really wise and kind. She was sitting on a leaf, enjoying the late afternoon sunshine.

"Hi there, Manny," she said without even looking up as if she knew he'd come by. "You look like something's bothering you."

"Is it that easy to tell?" Manny sighed, sitting down next to her. "I messed up, Gloria. I've been mean and not nice to others. Now I can't go to the Great Nectar Feast."

Gloria looked at him with her wise eyes. "So you're seeing how your actions have made others feel?"

"Yes," Manny said, "but I don't know how to make it right."

Gloria flapped her wings a little as she thought. "It's simple but not always easy, Manny. Being polite isn't just about rules; it's about showing you care for others. Saying 'please' and 'thank you,' waiting your turn, and listening when someone else is talking are ways we show we value each other. Little acts of kindness make a happy community."

Manny listened really carefully. He had never thought about being polite in this way. Gloria's words made him think differently. "You know, Manny," Gloria added, "it's never too late to change. You can become a good part of this community, but it will take some work and you have to really mean it."

Manny felt like a big weight had been lifted off him. For the first time in a while, he felt hopeful. "Thank you, Gloria," he said, and this time he really meant it.

"Go on now," Gloria gave him a little nudge. "You have a lot of making up to do, and the first step is up to you."

Feeling lighter and full of hope, Manny flew off toward the middle of the meadow. He was ready to try to fix the friendships he had hurt.

4

Feeling brave after talking to Gloria, Manny wanted to make things right. He got his chance pretty soon. The ants were making a line to carry leaves for their winter food, and Manny wanted to help.

"Can I help?" he asked. It felt weird to ask instead of just jumping in.

The ants looked at each other, not sure what to think. "Okay," said Andy the Ant, "could you grab that leaf over there?" Manny picked up the leaf and waited in line for his turn. He didn't push or complain. It was a small thing, but it felt really good.

His next chance to do better was at the Morning Dew Collection. This time, he didn't push to the front. He waited and when it was his turn, he took his share and said, "Thank you."

Sally the Spider was so surprised she

almost dropped her cup of dew. "You're welcome, Manny," she said, looking at him like he was a whole new bug.

Manny was trying hard, but old habits are tough to break. During a sing-along, he almost talked over Tina the Termite's solo part. But he stopped himself just in time, remembering what Gloria had told him about being respectful. It was a close one, and Manny felt a little embarrassed but also happy that he was getting better.

Soon, bugs started talking. "Have you noticed Manny acting different?" they whispered. "Maybe he's finally getting it."

People weren't sure what to think, but some were hopeful. Could Manny really become a nicer bug? And if he did, would they let him be part of the group again?

Manny felt people watching him, but he also felt their hope. This made him want even more to be a good part of the meadow's family.

- 5 -

The big day was here—time for the Great Nectar Feast! Even though Manny wasn't on the guest list, he went anyway. But he didn't want to ruin the fun; he wanted to make things better. He got to the spot where the special Golden Blossom flower was about to bloom.

All the bugs were buzzing and happy, but when Manny showed up, things got a little awkward. Just then, something happened.

The Golden Blossom started to open, but it got stuck on some vines. Oh no! Without the flower, there would be no special feast!

Manny saw what was happening and knew he could help. His long, skinny arms were just right for reaching in and his eyes were sharp for seeing through all the vines. But would the bugs let him?

Taking a deep breath and thinking about what he learned, he asked, "Can I try to help?"

Everyone went quiet. Then Benny the Butterfly said, "Yes, Manny. If you can help, please do."

Feeling really focused, Manny carefully wiggled his way through the vines. One by one, he untangled them from the Golden Blossom. Everyone was watching super closely. With one last tug, the vines let go and the flower popped open! It smelled amazing.

All the bugs started cheering. Manny did it! He helped save the feast, and he did it in a really nice way.

"Thank you, Manny," Benny said, flying over to him. "You didn't just save our special feast; you showed us that people can really change."

The other bugs started talking and they all agreed. Maybe, just maybe, Manny was becoming a better bug after all.

As the sun started to go down, making the meadow look all golden, everyone got ready to enjoy the feast by the Golden Blossom. Manny was standing a little bit away, not sure if he should join in.

Benny the Butterfly flew up to him. "Manny, why are you standing all alone? Come join us!"

"Really? Can I?" Manny asked, being super careful not to assume anything.

"Of course," Benny said with a big smile. "You've shown us that you've changed and that you care about us. You belong here now."

Hearing that made Manny feel so many feelings. This was the happy moment he had been hoping for but wasn't sure would ever come.

Walking up to the Golden Blossom, everyone moved aside to let him in. He took a tiny sip of the really yummy nectar. It wasn't just the taste that was sweet; the whole moment felt special.

"Manny, do you want to say something?" Benny asked him.

Manny cleared his throat and looked at all the faces around him. "I want to say thank you," he started, his voice sounding kind of emotional. "Thanks for giving me another chance. I'll be the best mantis—and the best friend—I can be."

All the bugs started cheering and clapping their little bug hands, or wings, or whatever they had! Manny felt proud and happy. He had not just become a part of the group again; he had also learned how important it is to be kind and respectful.

From that day on, Manny wasn't the rude mantis anymore.

He became a great example of how someone can change for the better. And so, everyone in the meadow lived happily and respectfully, now with one more good-mannered bug to make it even nicer.

- 7 -

As time passed, everyone in the meadow noticed how much Manny had changed. No more cutting in line, no more loud talking, and no more ignoring his friends. Manny was now super polite and kind!

He even started teaching the younger bugs about saying "please" and "thank you." Manny would tell them, "Good manners aren't just fancy words. They're how you show you care about your friends. And

when you care, great things happen!"
Everyone agreed: Manny was like a new
bug! He showed that saying nice words and
doing nice things makes everyone happier.

So, let's all remember Manny the Mantis's
story. It's never too late to change, and
being polite is like a magic key that makes
friends and opens up a whole world of fun.

And if anyone in the meadow ever forgets
to be polite, they just look at Manny. He

always remembers to be nice, and that helps everyone else remember, too.

The End

Made in the USA
Las Vegas, NV
04 November 2023

80180825R00020